Chasing
the
Sun

Written by the Masserman Brothers
Illustrated by Tammy Yee

CHASING IT ALL
PUBLISHING

For information regarding permissions, contact the publisher at:

Chasing It All Publishing
3846 Lower Honoapiilani Road, Unit 12
Lahaina, Hi 96761.
www.ChasingItAll.com

Authors: Mike, Oren, and Tal Masserman
Illustrator: Tammy Yee
Editor: Jennifer Thomas-Hayes

ISBN: 978-0-9995512-0-2

First Edition 2018
Published in the United States of America
Printed in the United States of America

To future generations—

Keep chasing it all...

Tiki the Turtle lived near the sea,
in a house made of rocks
and bright green algae.

On an island covered with coconut trees—
it had jungles and caves
and a warm ocean breeze.

Tiki spent days playing down by the beach,
where he felt like the sun
was just within reach.

But that sun would dip down,
night after night,
leaving only the glow
of the shining moonlight.

One night as the sun melted into the sea,
Tiki wondered where it went so curiously.

Did it go into the water to cool off and get a drink?
Well, that's what the sand crab told Tiki to think.

Could the sun possibly be
waiting to be found
in a place with sea horses
horsing around?

Or in a dark tunnel where nobody goes
among weird-looking creatures
with weird-looking toes?

"Is it on the other side?" Tiki needed to find out.

"I'm off on an adventure!"
he announced with a shout.

Tiki dove deep into the ocean, past fish of every color,
and then stopped to ask a starfish stargazing with his mother:

"Where does the sun go right after it sets,
when the sky turns pink and the day goes to rest?
Does it go upside-down or to the next town?
I've checked in the water. Can it be in the ground?"

"The sun's not here," he was told.
"It's back up on the sand.
Listen for the music of the pelican band."

Just as Tiki was reaching the shore,
he swam into dolphins,
dolphins galore.

Flipping and jumping and surfing the waves,
they even wore pink and white flower leis.

"Where is the sun?" Tiki asked.
"Do any of you know?"
"Into the jungle," they chattered,
"we think you should go!"

So off Tiki went through the leaning palm trees,
where he heard the squeaks
of swinging monkeys.

"Where does the sun go," he asked,
"at the end of the day?
Do any of you know—
is it so far away?"

"It must go up," they told him,
"to shine on the moon.
If you swing from this vine,
you'll see it soon."

So Tiki swung up,
amongst birds in the sky,
and was told by the toucans
and parrots flying by:

"The sun's not up here.
It's back down in the trees,
where the myna birds sing
with the sweet honeybees."

And so Tiki found the birds
they described.
As they gathered around
him, his eyes opened wide.

"Do any of you know
where the sun has gone?
Is it close by?
Should I continue on?"

"We saw the sun drift
into the bamboo forest,"
the myna birds whistled
in unison chorus.

Past creeks, waterfalls, and bamboo Tiki went.
He walked and he walked until his little legs were spent.

Huffing and puffing,
Tiki lay on the ground,
thinking, perhaps, he
should turn back around.

Just then he spotted a snail who was reading a book.
"Have you seen the sun? Tell me, where should I look?"

The snail smiled
    behind glasses too big for his face.
"The sun's a ball of gas
    ninety million miles from this place!
But...if you truly want to see the sun,
    up that mountain I think you should run."

Through the valley he went, and to the mountaintop.
Seeing an old gecko, he decided to stop.

"Hey, Mr. Gecko, have
you seen the sun?
Time's running out
and so far I have come."

"I've looked up, I've looked down, I've looked all around in search of the sun, which I still have not found."

The gecko rose slowly, like an old weathered oak,
and with the greatest of wisdom, these words he spoke:

"Some things will go up and some things will go down,
and yet other things are not meant to be found."

"But then there are things that always will rise.
Look out to the sea—you won't believe your eyes."

Off in the distance, out on the horizon...

There was the SUN,
magically rising!

"The sun's back up," Tiki said, "but where did it go?
I've been around the whole island and nobody knows."

"I know that you searched from dusk until dawn;
yet you never found out where the sun had gone.
But that's life," said the gecko, "And that's fine and okay.
Just look at the adventure you had along the way!"

"He's right!" Tiki laughed. He danced all the way down. He even passed sea horses horsing around.

And when he arrived
at the shores near his home,
he told his friends stories
of the places he'd roamed.

Lying in his hammock,
strumming his ukulele guitar,
he taught them the lessons
of his travels near and far.

Later that day as the sun went to sleep
and its purple rays glowed through the valley so deep,
Tiki smiled, because his journey had only begun...
He knew he would never stop chasing the sun.

Fun Facts

Sea Turtles

When fully grown, green sea turtles can weigh up to 700 pounds and can stay underwater for up to five hours.

Sea Horses

Sea horses are the slowest fish in the ocean—even though they flap their fins up to fifty times a second!

Starfish

Starfish can regrow lost limbs. It takes nearly a year for an arm to grow back.

Dolphins

Dolphins breathe through a blowhole on the top of their heads, not through their mouths. They talk to each other by whistling and clicking. A group of dolphins is called a pod.

Monkeys

Monkeys show they care by grooming each other, cuddling, and lip-smacking. They use their tails to swing from tree to tree. A group of monkeys is called a troop.

Myna Birds

Myna birds are very loud, vocal birds that mimic the sounds and songs of other birds.

Toucans

Toucans have the longest bills of nearly any bird in the world, which they use to reach deep into tree holes to grab food.

Sand Crabs

Sand crabs are excellent diggers, creating tunnels in the sand up to four feet deep. Their eyes allow them to see in front, behind, and on either side of them at all times. But they have a hard time seeing what's above them.

Geckos

Most geckos don't have eyelids, so they must clean their eyeballs with their tongues. Some geckos can change colors—called camouflaging—to hide in their surroundings. A gecko's feet are covered in tiny hairs that stick to surfaces, which allows them to scale trees and vines.

Snails

Snails are one of the slowest creatures on Earth. Thousands of tiny teeth located on their tongues help them to eat plants.

Visit www.ChasingItAll.com for more information!

About the Authors

The Masserman brothers grew up with an adventurous spirit
as they surfed, hiked, swung in hammocks,
and played ukulele music around the world.

They continue to chase the sun
from Maui, Phoenix, and San Francisco.

CPSIA information can be obtained
at www.ICGtesting.com
Printed in the USA
LVHW012127291220
675336LV00006B/27